Helpfulness for Hippos

Designed by Tabitha Blore
Edited by Lesley Sims
Design Manager: Nicola Butler

First published in 2023 by Usborne Publishing
Limited, 83-85 Saffron Hill, London
EC1N 8RT, United Kingdom. usborne.com

Hank

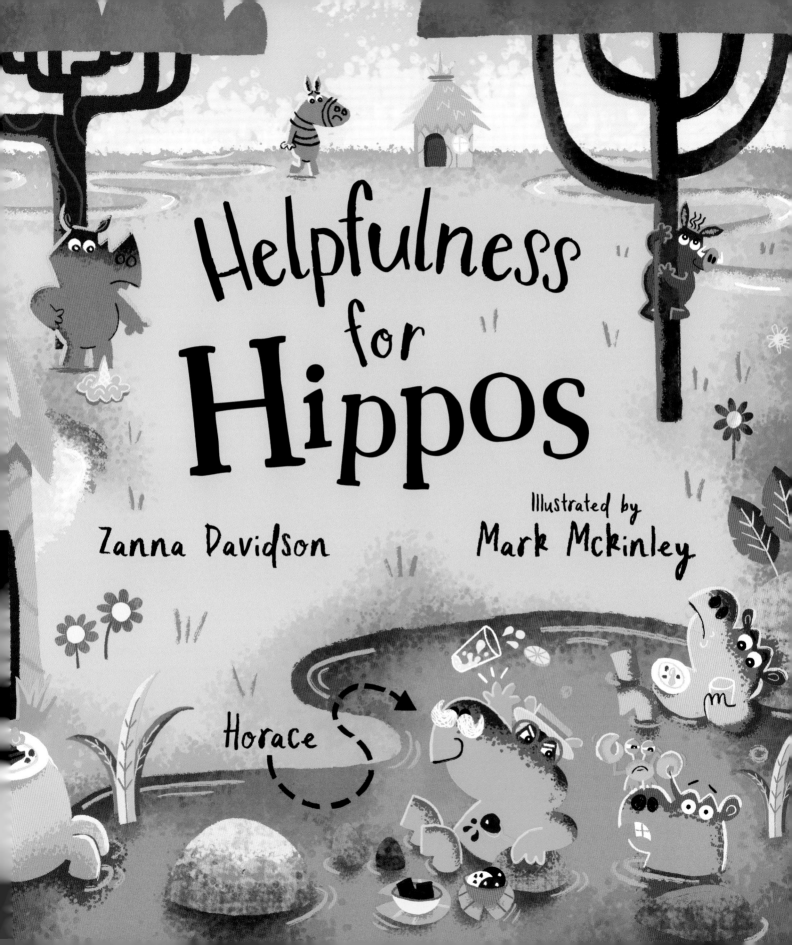

Helpfulness for Hippos

Zanna Davidson

Illustrated by
Mark Mckinley

Horace

If you go to the river **Limpopo**,
where frogs *ribbet* from bank to bank,

you're sure to find, he's one of a kind...

...a **hero** of a hippo named Hank!

He ferries old folk down the river.

He looks out for those on their own.

He lifts up his friends
if they're feeling low...

FIRST PRIZE
FOR BEING
HELPFUL

To Han
Thank yo
reading to

Monty Mo

...and **still** does the housework at home.

Not **all** the hippos look up to Hank.

Old Horace thinks Hank...

...is a FOOL!
Hippos aren't helpful!
It's not what we do!
We spend our time
sloshing in pools!

As for Hank – he's not **bothered** by Horace.

That hippo's just stuck in his ways!
Helping's THE BEST!
I don't want to rest!

"I'll keep helping for **all** of my days."

But that very night, it turns STORMY!
Rain gushes down from the sky.

It lashes the trees! It pours from the leaves!
The banks of the river grow high.

"Hank, save us!"
cry ten baby warthogs,
caught in the terrible flood.

Hank's there in a flash and carries them back,
safe through the rivers of mud.

"I'm trapped!" groans a gnarly old lion.
"Can anyone, **please**, get me out?"

"I'm coming!" shouts Hank and… BOSH!
He **smashes** him free with his snout.

Hank races to rescue a rhino,

and a herd of frightened gnu.

He saves a wet mole from a deep muddy hole,

and a flock of wet ostriches too.

But before he can leave the river,
along comes a tangle of trees.

They BONK poor Hank on his bottom,
then wallop him *oof!* on the knees.

Hank **yelps** for help!
But he's swept right away...

Oh no, he's gone over the EDGE!

"Yikes, I can't look! It's a

l
o
o
o
o
n
g
way down!"

Hank's friends are *longing* to help him.

Hank's size is a bit of a problem…
"He's so **BIG**!" says a worried baboon.

How can we pull him to safety?

Hank's got to be **double** our size!

We need help from the *un*helpful hippos.

Will that work?

We've just got to TRY!

The hippos all turn up their noses.
"Helping is **not** what we do!"
"Oh, you *must!*" plead the others, in anguish.

You know Hank
would do it
for YOU!

Horace has heard the commotion.
He feels a **jolt** of surprise,
for Hank's many acts of **kindness**
are flashing before his eyes.

Before Horace knows what he's doing,
he's up and about, all aquiver!
"We **must** help!" he says to the hippos.
"Come with me **now** to the river!"

All this time, I've been laughing at Hank...
Think of our life with him gone!
He's the glue that holds us together.
To leave him would simply be wrong.

The hippos all rally as they hear his cry.
One by one, they PLOP! from the bank.
"We've not helped before; who knows what's in store...
now it's OUR turn to save Hank."

They form a long chain
down the river...

...holding on,
nose to tail, in a line.

Horace reaches
for Hank...

There, I've got you!
Don't worry! You're going to be...

"Thank you!" says Hank, when he's back on the bank.
"Oh Horace! You came to my aid!"
"Well," Horace laughs, "I think we've found out,
this hippo can **still** change his ways."

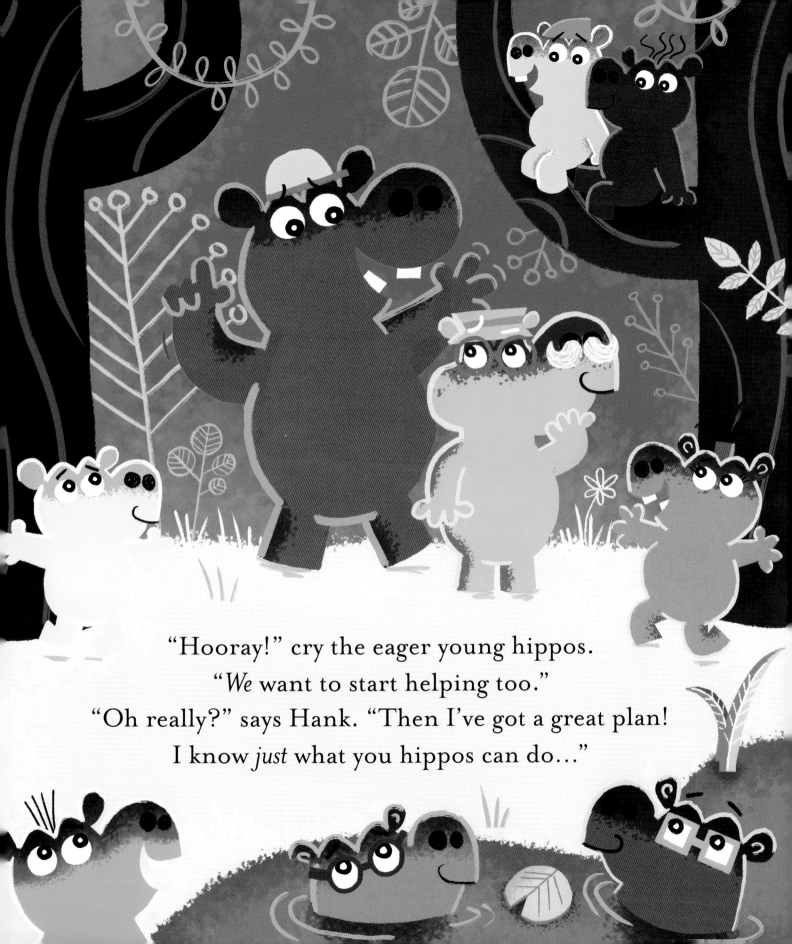

"Hooray!" cry the eager young hippos.
"*We* want to start helping too."
"Oh really?" says Hank. "Then I've got a great plan!
I know *just* what you hippos can do…"

Now by the river **Limpopo**,
where frogs **ribbit** from bank to bank,
you'll find lots of happy, young hippos…

...all learning to be
just like Hank!

As for **Horace** – he's still **very** lazy,
but willing to help *now and then*.
And Hank's learned to relax, just like Horace…

They've become the **greatest** of friends.